THE FUN BOOK OF SCARY STUFF

Emily Jenkins

PICTURES BY Hyewon Yum

Me

BULL TERRIER
the Bravest Dog EVER

PUG

FRANCES FOSTER BOOKS
Farrar Straus Giroux
New York

For Hazel and Ivy
—E.J.

To Frances
—H.Y.

Farrar Straus Giroux Books for Young Readers
175 Fifth Avenue, New York 10010

Text copyright © 2015 by Emily Jenkins
Pictures copyright © 2015 by Hyewon Yum
Color separations by Bright Arts (H.K.) Ltd.
Printed in China by Macmillan Production (Asia) Ltd.
(Supplier code 10), Kowloon Bay, Hong Kong
Designed by Roberta Pressel
First edition, 2015
1   3   5   7   9   10   8   6   4   2

mackids.com

Library of Congress Cataloging-in-Publication Data
Jenkins, Emily, 1967–
    The fun book of scary stuff / Emily Jenkins ; pictures by Hyewon Yum. — First edition.
        pages cm
    Summary: "A little boy tells his two dogs about all the things that scare him"—Provided by publisher.
    ISBN 978-0-374-30000-5 (hardback)
    [1. Fear—Fiction.   2. Dogs—Fiction.]   I. Yum, Hyewon, illustrator.   II. Title.
PZ7.J4134Fun 2015
[E]—dc23
                                                                                    2014040679

Farrar Straus Giroux Books for Young Readers may be purchased for business or promotional use.
For information on bulk purchases please contact Macmillan Corporate and Premium Sales Department
at (800) 221-7945 x5442 or by email at specialmarkets@macmillan.com.

Dad says I should make a list of everything that frightens me. He says it will help me be brave.

First, the stuff that frightens everybody.

MONSTERS.

Okay, fine. Stuff that definitely exists.

MY COUSIN JEMIMA.

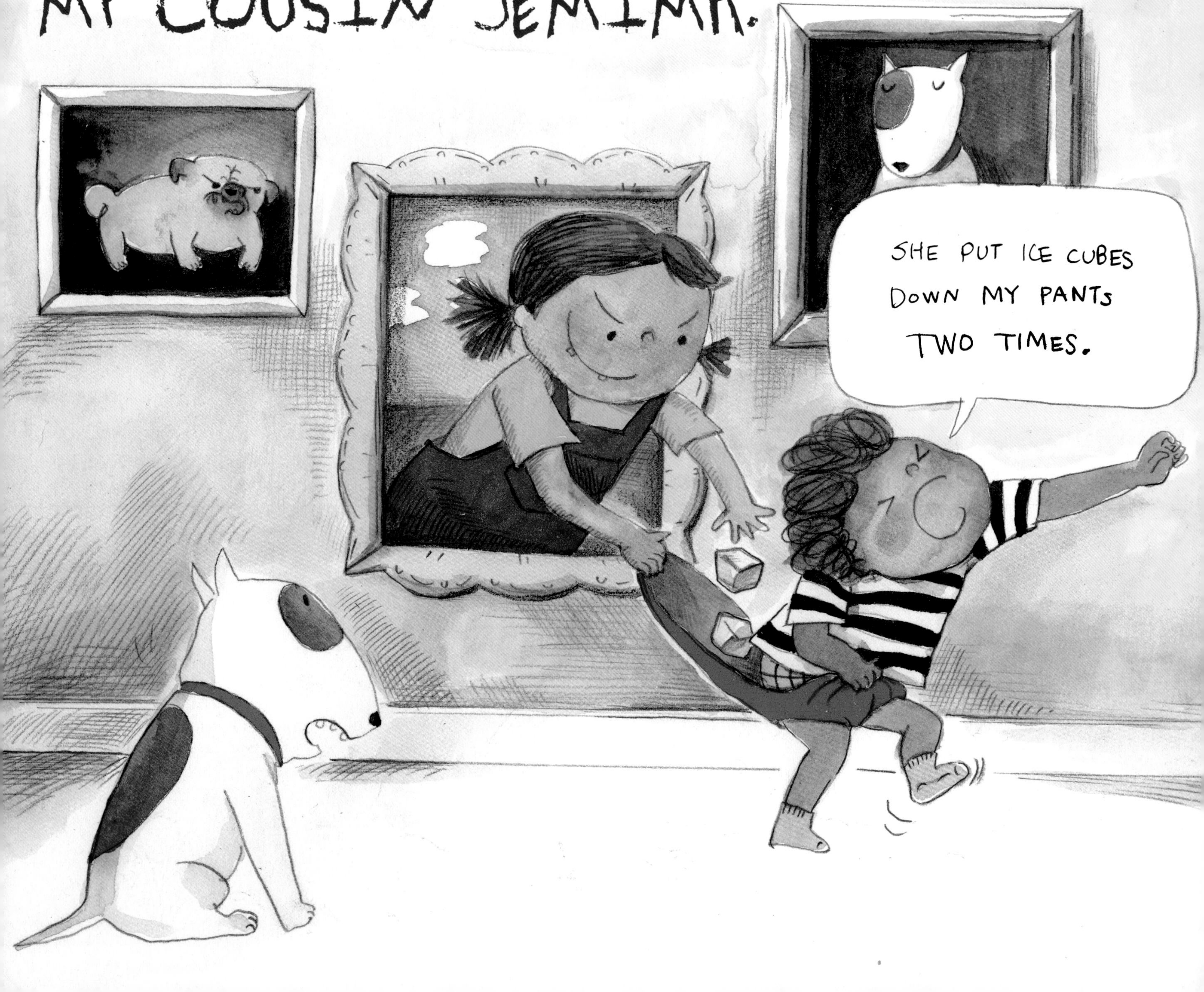

THE CROSSING GUARD BY SCHOOL.

SWIMMING POOLS.

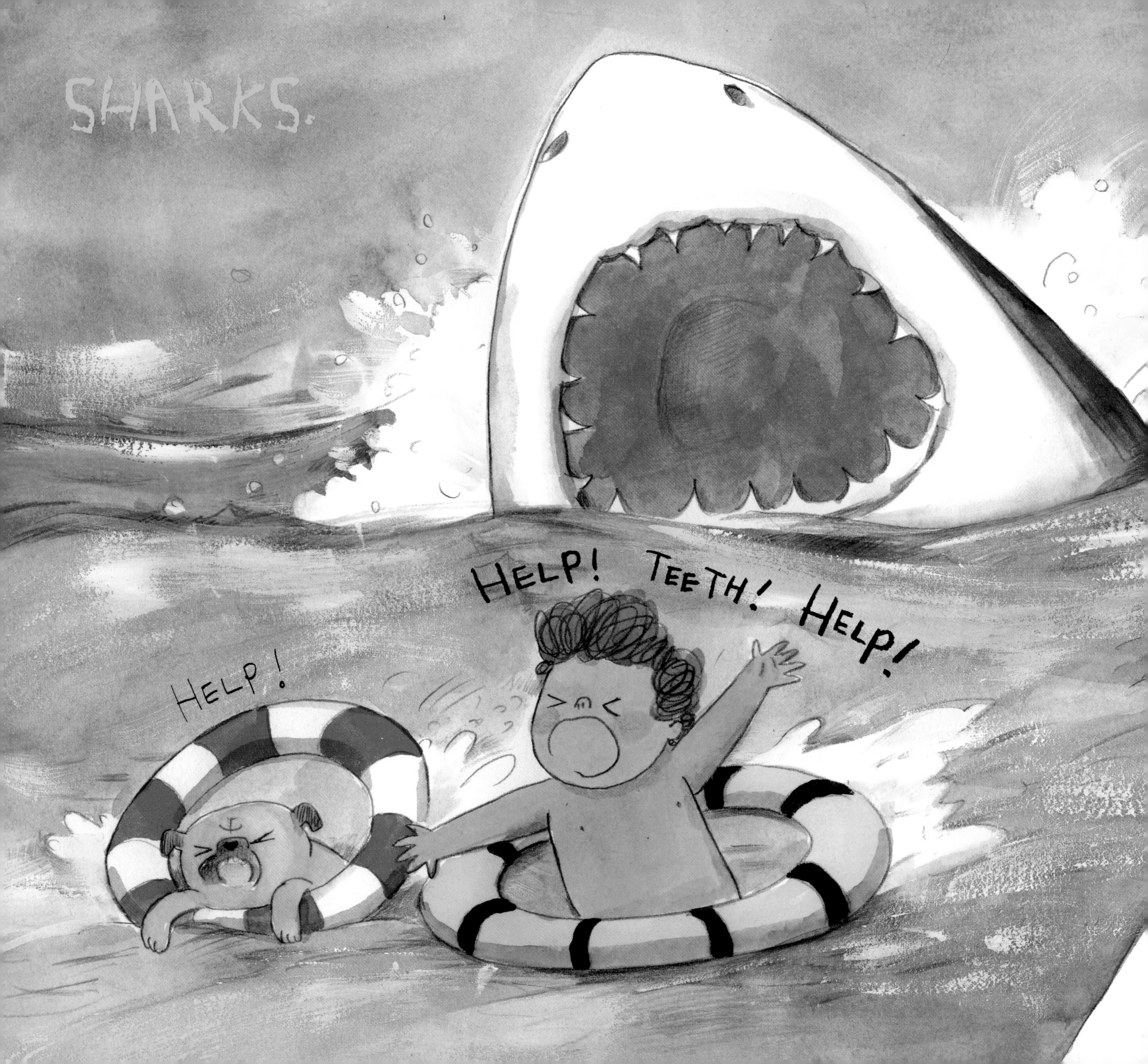
SHARKS.
HELP! TEETH! HELP!
HELP!

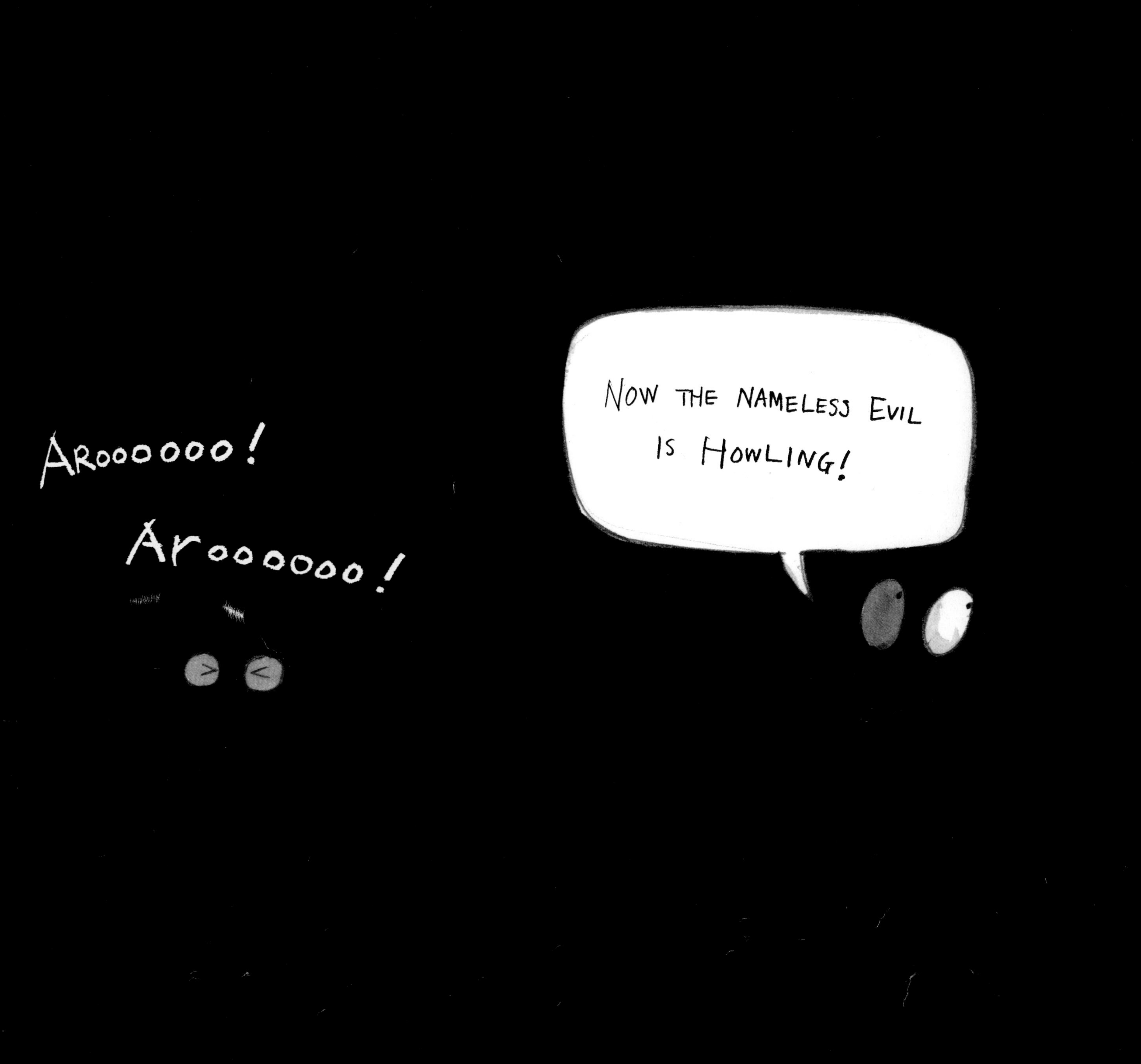

Arooooooo!
Arooooooo!
Now the nameless evil is howling!

You can turn on the light.